Elliott
the
Otter

The Totally Untrue Story of Elliott,
Boss of the Bay

Illustrated by John Skewes
Written by John Skewes and Eric Ode

little bigfoot

an imprint of sasquatch books
seattle, wa

Manufactured in China by C&C Offset Printing Co. Ltd. Shenzhen, Guangdong Province, in November 2014

Published by Little Bigfoot, an imprint of Sasquatch Books

20 19 18 17 16 15   9 8 7 6 5 4 3 2 1

Editor: Susan Roxborough
Project editors: Michelle Hope Anderson and Em Gale
Illustrations: John Skewes
Design: Joyce Hwang

Library of Congress Cataloging-in-Publication Data is available.

ISBN: 978-1-57061-952-6

Sasquatch Books
1904 Third Avenue, Suite 710
Seattle, WA 98101
(206) 467-4300
www.sasquatchbooks.com
custserv@sasquatchbooks.com

Ahoy, there!

I'm Elliott. Welcome to my bay. It's
a big, busy place, but nothing would
get done around here without me.

Here in my bay, everyone is going somewhere. Let me show you around. But stay close. The clock is ticking, and we have a lot to do.

Now here's someone I'm sure you'd like to meet.

This tugboat is a lot like me. He might not
be very big, but he has big responsibilities.

Straight ahead, now!
Keep it moving!

Barges and freighters from all over the world come to my bay. They arrive with giant containers filled with everything from books to chairs to teddy bears. Hardworking tugboats like this one bring them safely into the harbor.

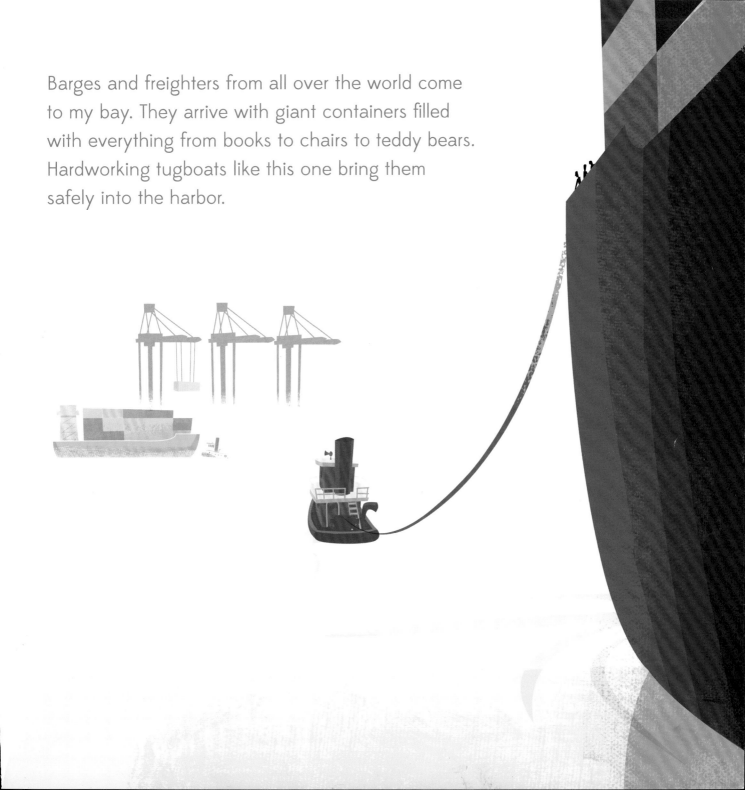

Here's where things really get busy.
Tall cranes unload the containers onto
trucks and long freight trains for delivery
across the country. Once the barges and
freighters are empty, we load them again
with outgoing cargo.

I give the signal, and soon they're back on their way, bringing products and materials from our country to ports around the globe.

Tugs and cranes, trucks and trains—in my bay, everyone has to do their part.

Hold on a minute. I'd better direct traffic. What would they do without me around here?

These hardworking ferryboats travel back and forth, back and forth across the water every day. They take cars, trucks, bicycles, and people from one place to another.

Jumping jellyfish, it's getting crowded up here! Take a deep breath. Let's see what's happening down below.

Hmm . . . My schedule says we should have guests arriving right about now. But the big guys like to take their own sweet time. They're never around when—

Yikes! There you are!

It's a big deal when the
orcas visit my bay.

Well, twist my whiskers. It looks like someone else is coming. Who could this be?

Is it time for the salmon already?

OK, *everyone, into the locks! Single file, nice and orderly.*

In my bay, everyone is going somewhere. But it seems these salmon are never satisfied. They began their lives in freshwater streams and rivers. Then, they swam out to the salty ocean. Today, they're heading back to their freshwater homes to spawn. If you're a boat or a salmon, traveling from the ocean to the fresh water means traveling through the locks.

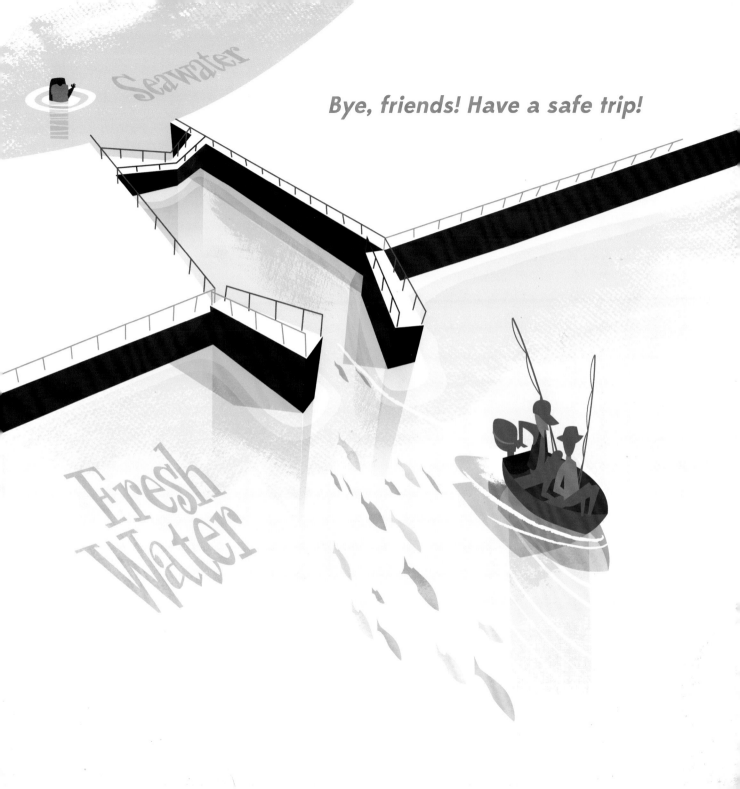

Oops! It looks like these salmon missed the locks. They're using the fish ladder instead. After all, when you can't take the elevator, use the stairs!

Hopping hermit crabs, is it that time already?

Let's get moving! We don't want to be late.

We made it! And we're just in time
for my most important job of all.
Hold on to your tail; here it comes!

Like I said, here in my bay, everyone
is going somewhere. Even me. After
dinner, I'm going to bed.

Tomorrow is another big, busy day.

Who Was the Real Elliott?

Elliott Bay was named by Lieutenant Charles Wilkes, who was commanding officer of the United States Exploring Expedition (1838–1842), but nobody really knows who "Elliott" was. There are some likely candidates:

Samuel Elliott
Midshipman

Jared Leigh Elliott
Chaplain

George Elliott
Ship's boy

Or . . .